To Luke:
    Merry Christmas!
        Love, Auntie Bonnie

The Trouble with DAD

For Joanna, Caroline and Rosie
(whose Dad also invents funny things!)

The Trouble with DAD

Babette Cole

G. P. Putnam's Sons   New York

The trouble with Dad

is his boring job.

If he didn't have such a boring job

he wouldn't spend all his spare time in
the shed making robots.

Mom nagged
Dad about
the robots.

They all went wrong . . . but that didn't stop him.

He made a robotic grass cutter.

He even made some robots to help in the house.

Mom went crazy!

He made a robotic hush-a-bye baby improver

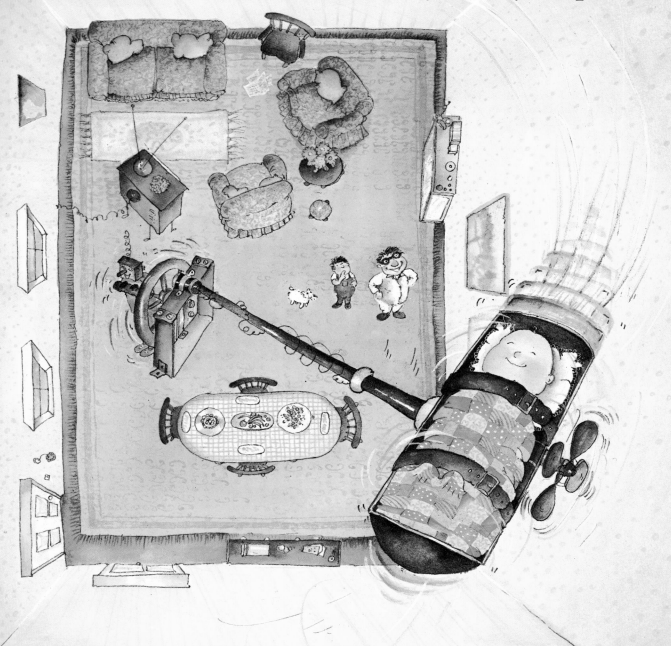

and one for seeing old ladies across the road.

Then there was the slimming robot

and the one for catching jewel thieves.

He made a whole soccer team of robots.
My friends and I challenged them to a match

but they were unbeatable.
They reached the playoffs!

Dad's robots became famous.

B.B.C.T.V.

They wanted to make a TV program about them.

But before the
camera crew
could start,
my baby
brother
found

the multi-laser-twister-operator.

When he started it up,
the robots went crazy all over town.

Luckily the little horror dropped it.

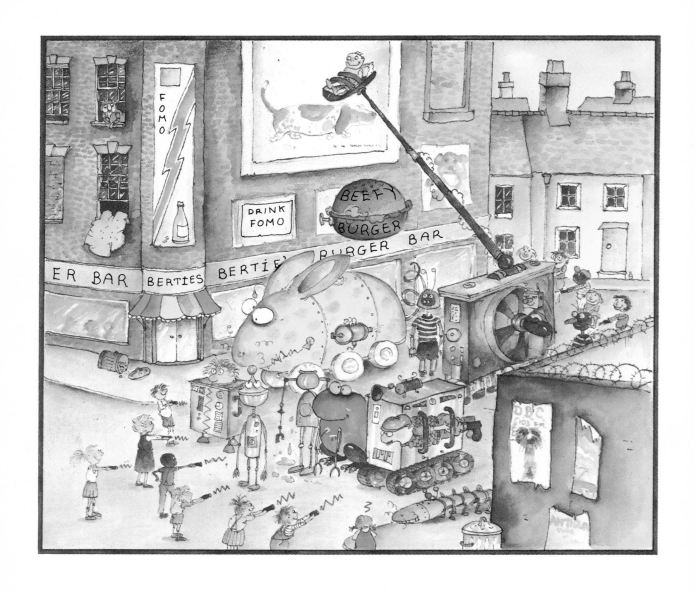

Then my friends and I rounded up
the robots for the program.

Dad had to pay
for all the damage.

A very rich man saw Dad's robots on TV.

He bought every single one of them.

Mom was delighted.

He put them in the desert in Arizona.

He called them works of art!

We got rich. Dad didn't have to do his boring job any more.

Now we both make robots.

Library of Congress Cataloging in Publication Data
Cole, Babette.
    The trouble with dad.
Summary: Dad's fantastic robot creations cause
the family to have incredible adventures.
[1. Robots—Fiction.   2. Inventors—Fiction.
3. Humorous stories]   I. Title.
PZ7.C6734Tp 1986   [E]   85-9563
ISBN 0-399-21206-X